KU-225-276

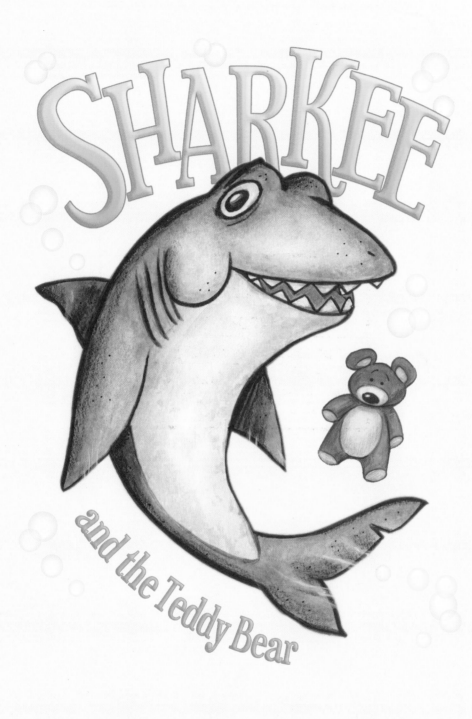

SHARKEE
and the Teddy Bear

Carrie Bolin and Jessica Firpi

Illustrated by John Graziano

Ripley
PUBLISHING

a Jim Pattison Company

Hey, what's that?

3 1513 40037632 8

CLACKMANNANSHIRE COUNCIL	
31513400376328	
Bertrams	23/01/2019
RIP	£6.99
CHI	JF

Copyright © 2018 by Ripley Entertainment Inc.

All rights reserved. Ripley's, Believe It or Not!, and Ripley's Believe It or Not!
are registered trademarks of Ripley Entertainment Inc. No part of this publication may be reproduced
in whole or in part, stored in a retrieval system, or transmitted in any form by any means, electronic,
mechanical, photocopying, recording, or otherwise, without written permission from the publisher.

First edition 2018
Library of Congress Control Number: 2017956677
ISBN 978-1-60991-208-6 (USA)
ISBN 978-1-78475-966-7 (UK)

10 9 8 7 6 5 4 3 2 1

Printed in China

This book was typeset in Athelas.
The illustrations were created traditionally
and in mixed media.
Book design by Rose Audette

Ripley Entertainment Inc.
7576 Kingspointe Parkway, Suite 188
Orlando, Florida 32819
Email: publishing@ripleys.com
visit us at www.ripleys.com/books

Young Arrow
20 Vauxhall Bridge Road
London SW1V 2SA

Young Arrow is part of the Penguin Random House
group of companies whose addresses can be found at
global.penguinrandomhouse.com.

Penguin
Random House
UK

First published in Great Britain in 2018
by Young Arrow

www.penguin.co.uk

A CIP catalogue record for
this book is available from
the British Library.

It looks like a teddy bear!

But, sharks don't need teddy bears...

Where did it go?

We decided to look for it.

We asked the blue lobster.

He wasn't very helpful.

The urchin, well, he didn't see anything.

The stingray wouldn't say.

The octopus was a little startled.

We didn't stay to chat.

And the boxer crab?

We didn't stand a fighting chance.

What if I *never* find the teddy bear?